Robert Louis Stevenson

# TREASURE ISLAND

TORMONT

# IN THE DAYS OF THE PIRATES...

*Ships, uniforms, and weapons of Britain's famous Royal Navy*

*Tall masts and big sails gave this ship great speed.*

Boatswain    Officer

Sailors

*Shotgun*

*Axe and naval
sword*

Sailors lifting the anchor by turning the winch
or capstan

Ships often had a beautifully carved
wooden statue on the prow or front
of the ship. It was called a figure-
head. This one belonged to a 17th-
century ship of the British Royal
Navy.

*Loading and firing a cannon was a dangerous job.*

# THE AUTHOR: ROBERT LOUIS STEVENSON

*Robert Louis Stevenson is one of the best-loved story-tellers in the English language. He was 33 years old when he suddenly became famous with the publication of* **Treasure Island**.

*Stevenson was born in Edinburgh, Scotland, in 1850. Although he became a lawyer to please his parents, he never practised law. He had an adventurous spirit and a gift for telling stories. Soon he was traveling in Europe and America, writing articles, stories, and poems for magazines.*

*Readers young and old were delighted with* **Treasure Island,** *the story of a young boy who goes in search of pirate treasure buried on a Caribbean island.*

*In his many books, Stevenson created action-packed adventure stories and a series of memorable characters. One of the most famous is Long John Silver, the wicked pirate leader in* **Treasure Island**.

*He seemed to be able to write almost anything: historical adventures like* **Kidnapped, The Black Arrow, The Master of Ballantrae,** *and* **David Balfour;** *poetry like* **A Child's Garden of Verses** *for young children; and even horror stories like* **The Strange Case of Dr. Jekyll and Mr. Hyde**.

*Stevenson had tuberculosis, and in 1891 he settled in the warm Samoan Islands in the South Pacific. There he stayed, still writing, until he died in 1894. He was 44 years old. The Samoans respected and admired him, and called him "Tusitalia," the teller of tales.*

# The Old Sailor

In the days when my father was keeper of an old inn called the 'Admiral Benbow,' near Bristol, we had a strange visitor.

He came slowly to the door, pulling a wheelbarrow with a sailor's chest on it. His hands were very dirty, his face was very brown, and he had an ugly swordscar on his cheek.

As he walked, he sang an old sea song:

*Fifteen men on the dead man's chest –*
*Yo-ho-ho, and a bottle of rum!*

He called for a glass of rum as soon as he came into the inn, and asked gruffly if we had many people staying there.

"No sir," said I.

He seemed pleased, and said he would be staying a while. He gave a few gold coins as payment in advance. He told us to call him "captain", but to me he was always the Brown Man, because of his brown face.

Our guest was a silent fellow. He would wander along the shore during the day, clutching his brass telescope. In the evening, he would sit by the fire in the bar, drinking rum. If other guests spoke to him, he would answer roughly and begin singing his song.

When he first arrived, the captain said he would give me four pennies every month if I would watch out for a one-legged sailor. I was to run and tell him if ever such a man appeared.

One January morning, the captain rose earlier than usual and went for his usual walk along the shore. As I was setting the table for breakfast, a thin man with an evil face wandered in.

"Who will be sitting at this table?" asked the newcomer. "My old friend, Bill Bones, perhaps?"

I said that I knew no one by that name, and that I was setting the table for the captain, who was out walking.

"Calls himself captain, does he?" the newcomer growled, moving to the wall by the door. He waited there, glancing furtively out the door every now and then.

At last, the captain returned from his walk and sat down at the table.

# THE FIGHT

No sooner was the captain seated than the stranger stepped forward.

"Bill, don't you recognize me?" he asked, grinning wickedly. "Surely you haven't forgotten your old friend Black Dog?"

The captain jumped up, knocking over his chair. He pulled out a knife, and in a flash the two men were fighting. The captain fell to the ground, and Black Dog raced out of the inn.

Luckily, our friend Dr. Livesey arrived at that moment for his daily visit to my father, who was very ill. He said the captain wasn't hurt, and just needed rest.

Later, I took the medicine ordered by the doctor up to the captain's room. He tried to get out of bed, but he was too weak.

"Look out, Jim," he said to me. "Those fellows are after me. They'll try to give me the black spot for sure. You keep a sharp eye out for that one-legged man, do you hear?"

I would have told my mother all this, but my father died very soon after that. The captain seemed to get better, but he was a changed man. He would stick his nose out now and then to smell the sea, then come right back in. His moods grew worse and worse.

One day I noticed another stranger coming toward the inn. He must have been blind, because he felt his way with a cane, going tap-tap-tap, and wore a shade over his eyes.

"Can anyone tell me if I'm near the 'Admiral Benbow'?" he called. I answered, and he asked me to give him a hand. As soon as I came near him, he grasped my arm painfully.

"Take me to see my friend Bill," said this dreadful man.

We walked into the inn. "Here's a friend for you, captain," I said.

The captain turned as white as a sheet.

"Come on, Bill, give us a hand. Here, boy, take his wrist and bring it near mine."

I obeyed, and I saw him hand something to the captain.

"Well, that's done," said the blind man. He tap-tapped his way out of the inn with amazing skill, and disappeared.

The captain was in a state of shock. I let go of his wrist, and he immediately opened his hand and looked carefully at his palm. "At ten o'clock!" he shouted. "We've got six hours!"

The captain was in a state of shock. I let go of his wrist, and he immediately opened his hand and looked carefully at his palm. "At ten o'clock!" he shouted. "We've got six hours!"

He leapt to his feet, swayed a bit, and clutched at his throat. The next thing I knew, he'd fallen flat on his face.

I bent over him, but he didn't seem to be breathing. In fact, as Dr. Livesey told us afterward, he had died of a stroke.

I raced upstairs to tell my mother that the captain was dead. Then I told her the rest of my story, too. We decided to run to the next village to ask for help, as we were alone in the inn.


# THE BLACK SPOT


"But he owed me a lot of money," said my poor mother. And so she decided that we would take what was owing first.

I knelt by the body and found a circle of paper, blackened on one side. On the other side was written, "You have until ten o'clock tonight." This must have been the black spot he'd talked about.

At that moment the clock chimed. It was six in the evening.

I took the captain's keys, and we went upstairs to open his trunk. On top were some clothes. On the bottom was a package wrapped in oilskin, and a canvas bag filled with coins.

"I'll only take what he owed me, and not a penny more," said my mother.

We began to count out the coins. Before we were halfway through, I heard a sound that made my heart jump. From the road came the tap-tap-tap of a cane.

Suddenly there was a bang on the inn door, then a long silence.

The tapping started again, then faded away. Then we heard a low whistle. I begged my mother to take everything and run.

"I'll take what I have," she said, jumping to her feet.

"And I'll take this to make up for the rest," said I, picking up the oilskin packet. A minute later we were out on the road.

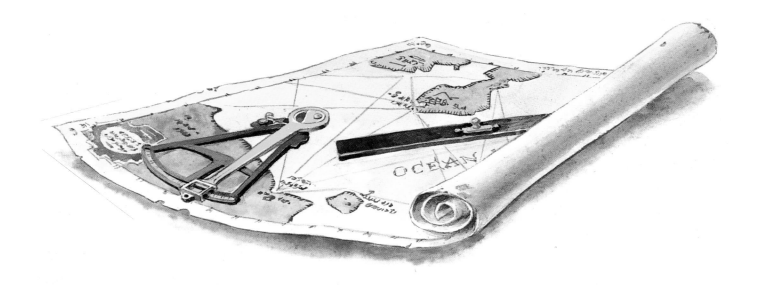

"I think I'm going to faint," said my mother. Sure enough, she gave a sigh and fell on my shoulder. I dragged her off the road and behind a bush, just in time. Our enemies arrived and I could hear the blind man's voice.

"Down with the door!" he cried.

"Aye, aye, sir," answered the others.

They seemed surprised to find the door open. Then I heard a muttering, as though they were discussing something.

"Bill's dead, Pew!" one of the men announced.

"Search him, then get the chest," ordered the blind Pew.

There was a pause, and then a voice shouted from an upstairs window. "Someone's been here first. There's a bit of money, but Flint's map is gone!"

"It's those people at the inn, probably that boy. Scatter, men, and find them!"

At that moment, I heard the low whistle again, followed by the sound of hoofbeats. This saved us, for the men ran off, leaving Pew stranded in the middle of the road. In the confusion, he started running toward the sound of the riders just as they came galloping into view. The first horse trampled him before its rider could do a thing.

I jumped out onto the road and hailed the horsemen. They were customs officers. Someone had reported a smuggler's boat down in the cove.

"And a lucky thing for you, Jim Hawkins," said one of the officers when I told him about our trouble. The officers took my mother to a house in the village. As for me, I was taken to see Dr. Livesey, who was having dinner at Squire Trelawney's house.

# THE TREASURE MAP

"Let's open that oilskin packet," said Dr. Livesey when I had told him about our adventure. He cut open the cover and pulled out a book and a roll of paper sealed with lumps of red wax. The book seemed to be a captain's account book, with a list of ships that had been sunk.

"Why, it's clearly a pirate ship's log!" exclaimed the squire.

Dr. Livesey and I leaned over the squire's shoulder as he carefully removed the seals from the paper and unrolled it.

It was a map of an island, shaped a bit like a fat dragon standing upright. It showed two good harbors, something called "The Stockade," a hill in the center marked "The Spyglass," and three crosses in red ink. Beside one cross was written, "bulk of treasure here." On the back were some instructions and the signature, "J.F."

"That must be for 'Flint'," I said, remembering how the thieves had talked about "Flint's map."

"The famous Captain Flint!" cried the squire. "Doctor, we're going treasure hunting. I'll leave for Bristol tomorrow, and in three weeks we'll have a ship of our own. You'll be the ship's doctor, and Jim can be our cabin boy. We'll take my servants, Redruth and Hunter, and I'll find a crew for us."

"Squire, we'll go," said Dr. Livesey. "But you'd better tell no one about that map, or those scoundrels will be on our trail. I'm sure they wouldn't hesitate to slit our throats for it."

The squire set off for Bristol the next day. We soon had a letter saying he'd bought a ship called the *Hispaniola*. He'd hired a one-legged innkeeper called Long John Silver as ship's cook, and this man had obligingly helped him get a crew together.

I said goodbye to my mother, who was back at our inn again. The squire had paid to have everything repaired, and had found someone to help her while I was gone. The next day I took the stagecoach to Bristol, feeling very excited.

"Well, we're nearly ready," said Squire Trelawney when I arrived. He was dressed in a smart blue coat, like a ship's officer, and was doing his best to walk like a sailor.

I was sent with a message to Long John Silver's inn. It was a cheerful, clean little place, and the customers were mostly seafaring men. I was a little anxious about meeting Long John. Of course, the squire's description of a one-legged man had reminded me of the dead captain's fears.

Long John hopped about with a crutch, his left leg being cut off at the hip. He was very tall and strong, with an intelligent, smiling face. One look was enough to tell me that this was no pirate. No one could have been less like the blind Pew or Black Dog.

"So you're our cabin boy!" he said to me in a friendly way.

I was about to reply when who should I see, making for the door, but Black Dog!

"Stop him!" I cried. "That's Black Dog!"

"I don't care who he is – he hasn't paid his bill," retorted Long John. He sent two men after Black Dog. They soon came back, saying they'd lost his trail.

"A rascal like that in my inn!" Long John said when I explained who Black Dog was. "Whatever will Squire Trelawney think?"

This reminded me about the squire's note. I gave it to Long John, and a few minutes later we set off for the inn where the squire was staying.

# Setting Sail for Treasure Island

As we walked along, Long John told me all about the ships in the harbor, the men who worked in them, the kind of cargo they carried, and where they sailed. I had never gone much beyond the little cove near my mother's inn, and was spellbound by his tales of the sea.

We went aboard the *Hispaniola*, where we found the squire and Dr. Livesey. I was introduced to Mr. Arrow, the first mate, and the ship's captain, Mr. Smollet.

Captain Smollet was clearly bothered about something. "I must speak to you gentlemen," he said to the squire and Dr. Livesey. "There's been some talk among the crew about you having a map of an island where treasure is buried. They seem well informed – even know the latitude and longitude of its location."

Dr. Livesey looked at the squire.

"I never told a soul!" protested the squire. The doctor didn't look convinced.

"Never mind how they found out," said Captain Smollet. "The fact is, they know why you're making this voyage. The first mate isn't strict enough with the men, and I don't like the look of things. I didn't choose this crew, as you know.

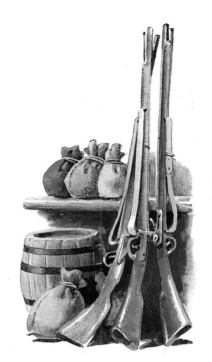

"I advise you to move the gunpowder and weapons to the hold beneath my cabin. Your servants should sleep near our quarters, and not with the crew. As long as these men don't know who actually has the map, we're reasonably safe."

Dr. Livesey admired the captain's frankness, but the squire wasn't a bit pleased. He was used to having things his own way. However, there can't be two captains on a ship, and the squire had to agree to the suggested change.

It took some time to move the gunpowder and weapons. We had to wait a day longer before sailing. I worked hard under Captain Smollet's strict eye. By the end of the day I disliked him as much as the squire did.

Just before dawn the next day, the first mate blew his whistle and all hands went on deck. Sleepy though I was, I watched everything that was going on. It was all so new and interesting! The men began to turn the wheel that lifted the anchor.

"Give us a song mates!" cried one sailor.

"How about this one?" said Long John Silver, and he began to sing:

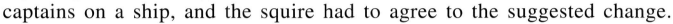

*Fifteen men on the dead man's chest...*

The entire crew responded with, *"Yo-ho-ho, and a bottle of rum!"*

The wheel turned, the anchor rose out of the water, and the ship began to move as its sails filled with the breeze. We were off!

I stood at the bow of the ship for an hour, feeling the wind in my face and watching the waves. Finally, I went to my cabin and was soon fast asleep.

Our voyage began happily enough, but after a while things began to get difficult. For one thing, Mr. Arrow, the first mate, began to appear on deck in the evening with very red eyes. He mumbled instead of talking clearly, and staggered so much that sometimes he could hardly stand up.

No one was much surprised when he disappeared one stormy night.

"Must have fallen overboard," said the captain. "Well, at least he's saved me the trouble of putting him in the brig." This was the captain's way of referring to the ship's prison cell.

Job Anderson, our boatswain, took Arrow's place as first mate.

I used to spend a lot of time talking to Israel Hands, the coxswain. He was a good friend of Long John Silver and he called him "Barbecue" – something I never dared to do.

"Barbecue is a fine man," Hands would say. "He has studied a lot. He talks like a printed book, you know." However, all I knew was that Long John treated me kindly and was always glad to see me in his kitchen, which we called the ship's galley.

"Come here, Hawkins," he would say as he hopped about, "come and have a chat with old John Silver. Here's Cap'n Flint – that's my parrot, named in memory of the old buccaneer. Going to be a mighty good voyage, isn't that so, Flint?"

"Pieces of eight, pieces of eight!" the parrot would squawk, until Long John covered his cage with a piece of cloth.

In the meantime, Captain Smollet and Squire Trelawney were still grumbling about each other to Doctor Livesey.

The squire had his own ideas about how to treat the crew. If we had bad weather, or if it were someone's birthday, the squire would order a double ration of rum for the sailors.

"No good will come of spoiling the men," the captain would mutter.

What bothered the captain most was the barrel of apples placed on deck for the sailors. They could help themselves whenever they wanted.

"They'll start thinking they can help themselves to whatever they like," he said.

But something good came of that apple barrel. Without it, we might have all been murdered by the crew.

One day, as the sun was going down, I felt very hungry and went to get an apple. The big barrel was almost empty, and I had to climb right inside to get at the fruit.

## THE APPLE BARREL

We were nearing the end of our journey. The men were all busy with their chores, or watching out for the island.

Everything was quiet except for the rocking of the boat and the swish of the sea as we sailed along. I curled up at the bottom of the barrel and fell asleep.

Suddenly the barrel was given a rough shake that woke me up. Someone had sat down on the deck and was leaning against my hiding place. I was about to jump out when I heard Long John's voice. Before he had said a dozen words, I knew that the lives of all the good men on board depended on me. I crouched in the barrel, shivering with fear.

"No," Long John was saying, "Flint was the captain. I was the quarter-master, because of my one leg. I lost that from the same cannon ball that blinded old Pew."

"Those must have been adventurous times," said another voice that I recognized. It was Dick, the youngest sailor.

"I sailed first with Captain England. A fine buccaneer, he was! Then with Flint," continued Long John. "This time I'm on my own, you might say."

And then he began to explain how he'd saved nine hundred pounds from England's voyages and two thousand from Flint's. "Not bad for a common sailor – and all safe in the bank," he said. "Not like old Pew, who spent all his share in a week and was a beggar after that."

It made me sick to hear how Long John praised the life of a pirate. He told Dick of the money to be made by attacking ships, stealing the cargo, and murdering everyone aboard.

"And as for our present plans," Long John added, "you can trust the whole crew, because they know and fear me. Even old Flint was afraid of me."

Now I heard Israel Hands' voice. "Let's kill the squire and his friends right now, beginning with the captain."

"No, we need the captain to sail the ship, because we common sailors don't know how to navigate properly," said Long John. "It's better to wait until they find the treasure and get it back on the ship. Then we'll take our chances and sail the ship ourselves."

# TREASURE ISLAND

Just at the moment, a voice yelled out, "Land! Land ahoy!" I heard a lot of feet clattering across the deck. Without a moment's thought, I tumbled out of my barrel and rushed up to the bow of the ship.

The moon had come out. To the southwest I could see three hills poking up above the horizon. Behind me, I heard Captain Smollet's voice.

Men," said the captain, "have any of you ever seen that land?"

"I have, sir," replied Long John. "I stopped there once when I was a cook on a trading ship."

"Is the harbor to the south?" asked the captain.

"Yes, protected by a small island – Skeleton Island, it's called, because pirates once used it. That's Foremast Hill to the north, on the main island, and Mizzenmast Hill to the south. The big one in the middle is Spyglass Hill. Pirates used to use it as a lookout."

"Look at this map," said the captain. "Is that the place?"

Long John's eyes lit up. It was a copy of our treasure map, but without a single red X on it, or any notes.

"Yes, sir," said the cook, hiding his disappointment. He told the captain about the currents in the sea around the island, and the best way of approaching the harbor. I was amazed to hear Long John admit he knew anything about the island.

While this was going on, I found Dr. Livesey. "Doctor," I whispered, "get the captain and the squire aside. I've got some terrible news."

The doctor didn't blink an eye, but walked calmly over to the captain and began to chat.

A few moments later, the captain announced to the crew that we'd reached our destination. "Double rum rations for all," he said.

"Come gentlemen," he added to the doctor and the squire. "Let's drink a toast in my cabin." A short while later, he sent for me.

"Now then, young Hawkins, speak up," said Captain Smollet.

I told them everything I'd heard while in the apple barrel. The three men sat very still and didn't take their eyes off me.

"Well, Captain, you were right," said Squire Trelawney.

"I think we still have some loyal men, plus your own servants," replied the captain. "We'll work out a plan of action to defend ourselves, and Jim can warn us of anything suspicious."

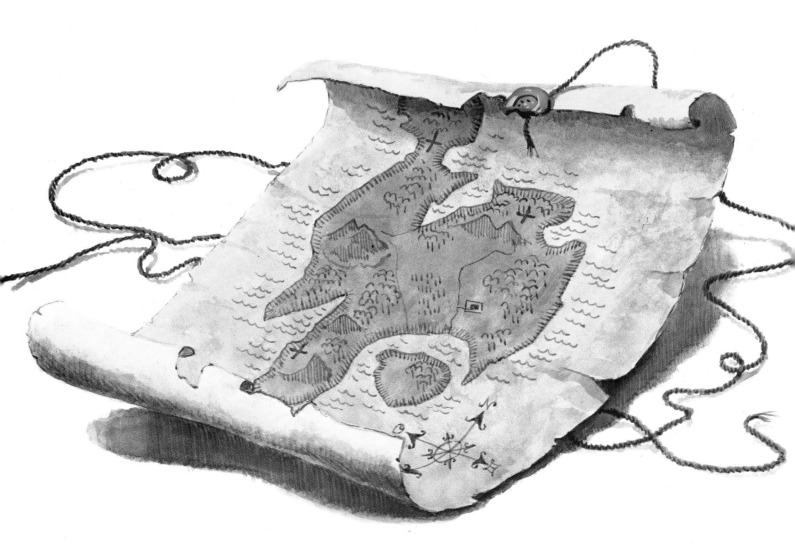

# My Shore Adventure

When I came on deck next morning, the view had changed completely. In front of us was an island covered by greyish-colored trees and patches of yellow sand. The three hills stuck up like huge, bare rocks. It looked all very sad – not a bit like the island I'd imagined.

Our ship creaked and groaned as sails and masts strained in the wind. We had to take the ship around the corner of the island.

The sailors were busy letting the sails out or pulling them in, and I had to help prepare the lifeboats so that we could go ashore once we'd anchored. The heat was terrible, and the men complained a lot.

Long John stood next to the man steering the ship, and at last we slipped past Skeleton Island and into the harbor. There, we dropped anchor.

We were surrounded by beaches and marshy land on two sides, with Skeleton Island on the third. From the marshes came a swampy smell.

The doctor wrinkled his nose. "I'll bet my wig there's malaria here," he said.

The sailors were becoming more restless by the minute. Even those we thought were honest men seemed to catch the unsettled mood. Strangely enough, Long John seemed to be doing his best to calm them down.

The captain quietly spoke to the rest of us, and we went down to his cabin and held a council of war.

"Squire," said the captain, "if I give one more order to the crew, we'll have a mutiny on our hands. The only man we can trust to keep the men calm is Long John Silver himself. He understands how to get them in a better mood – until he's ready to attack, that is.

"I propose we give the crew permission to go ashore for the afternoon. If they accept, we'll have the ship for our fortress. If none of them go, we'll have to defend ourselves in this cabin."

All the trustworthy men were given loaded pistols. The captain went up on deck and told the crew they could go ashore and have a look around the island. The men cheered. I think the silly fellows thought they'd trip over treasure as soon as they set foot on dry land!

John Silver organized the landing party. Six sailors would stay on the ship and thirteen would go ashore. A cannon shot at six o'clock would be the signal to come back.

It was then that I got one of the wild ideas that were to help save us. Why not go ashore myself? Before I knew it, I had slipped over the side of the ship and into the nearest lifeboat.

Long John had spotted me, just the same, and I began to feel rather nervous. As we reached land, I grabbed an overhanging branch and swung myself onto the shore.

"Jim, Jim!" called Long John, but I shot off into the underbrush, thrilled with the idea of being a real explorer.

A wild duck flew up with a nervous quack, but I saw no sign of any human inhabitant. After a bit, however, I heard voices. I crawled in their direction. Long John was talking to a crew member named Tom.

He was trying to convince him to join the mutiny. Tom would have nothing to do with it. "I can't believe you'd get involved."

Before he could finish, a horrible scream rose from a distance.

Tom jumped up, but Long John didn't bat an eyelash. "I reckon that'll be Alan," he said. Alan had been one of the loyal members of the crew.

"So you've killed Alan! Well, kill me too, if you can!" Tom turned his back and began to walk away. Poor Tom didn't get far. Long John hurled his crutch and knocked him down. He hopped over to his victim and buried a knife in Tom's chest.

My head was whirling with the horror of what I'd just seen. The murderer calmly wiped his knife, then took out a whistle and blew a few short blasts.

# THE MYSTERIOUS MAN

That was enough for me. I crawled away as fast as I could, then ran blindly. At last I found myself on a slope. Tall pines grew here, and the air smelled fresh.

Suddenly a shower of stones came rattling down the slope. I stopped in my tracks. There, behind the trunk of a pine, was a dark, shaggy figure. I couldn't tell if it was a bear, a man, or a monkey.

Facing Long John would be better than this, I thought. I turned to go back the way I'd come. But as I moved along, the creature flitted from tree to tree. Was it a cannibal?

At this moment, I remembered that I had a pistol with me. The creature was a man, at least. I took a deep breath, and walked straight toward him.

All at once, the strange man jumped out from behind a tree and threw himself on his knees. His face was very sunburnt, and he wore clothes made from the tatters of an old sail.

"Who are you?" I asked in amazement.

"Ben Gunn – marooned on this island for three years!"

"Marooned!" I exclaimed. I knew this meant he'd been left behind as a punishment by some pirate.

"I've lived on wild goat's meat, berries, and oysters ever since then. By the way, do you happen to have some cheese?"

Ben told me he'd been with Captain Flint's ship when the treasure was buried. Ben had come back later, bringing some other men. "After twelve days of digging," he explained, "they were so disgusted with me that they sailed away and left me on this island with only a shotgun, a spade, and a pickaxe."

He looked at me curiously. "Say, is that Flint's ship in the harbor?"

"No, but some of Flint's men sailed with us, and it looks like there'll be trouble. I don't know how I'll get aboard again." Then I told him about the squire and the doctor.

"If I helped you, do you think the squire would make sure I wasn't punished for being one of Flint's men? I'd want a share of the treasure, of course."

All this time, Ben was steering me through the trees.

"What's that?" he asked suddenly. At that moment, although it was well before six, the roar of a cannon echoed all over the island.

"They've begun to fight!" I shouted. "Follow me!" I started running toward the ship.

Ben kept up with me easily, chattering the whole time. As we got closer to the beach, we heard another shot, followed by the sputter of pistols. "Left, keep left, stay under the trees!" Ben Gunn kept telling me. Suddenly, not too far ahead, I saw the Union Jack fluttering above the trees!

# DR LIVESEY CONTINUES
## THE STORY

It was Hunter, the squire's servant, who brought the news about Jim. The boy had gone ashore with the others. We ran up on deck, very much afraid for his safety.

We could see the two boats pulled up on the shore, just where a river ran out from the marsh. There was a man guarding each one, but the rest of the sailors had disappeared.

Hunter and I decided to go ashore. We steered our lifeboat away from the others, and around a point of land. There, out of sight, we came ashore. Hunter stayed with the boat, and I started walking through the trees, trying not to make any noise.

Before I had gone a hundred yards, I found myself in front of a high picket fence – the stockade marked on our map! It surrounded a little hill. Someone had built a solid log house on top of the hill.

I climbed over the stockade and inspected the house. It was big enough for forty men, and had small holes in the walls for shooting at attackers.

What pleased me most about this pirate fort was the spring. A little well had been made around it. With water and a good supply of food and ammunition, you could hold off a regiment. What was more, we were running low on fresh water on the ship.

I was thinking this over, when suddenly a horrible cry rang out over the island. "Jim Hawkins is done for," was my first thought. I raced back to the shore and jumped into the waiting boat. "Row for you life!" I shouted to Hunter.

Our friends on board were pretty shaken. By this time I had a plan. Placing Redruth on guard against the six sailors still on board, Hunter and I began loading food and ammunition into the lifeboat. How wise Captain Smollet had been when he made us store things in the hold underneath his cabin!

Hunter and I then rowed back to the shore as before. I saw one of Long John's boat guards run into the forest.

Luck was with us, however. We landed safely and got all our stores into the stockade. I left Hunter on guard, and rowed back to the ship as fast as I could.

Now even the squire helped me load, tossing things out the cabin window. What we didn't have room for, we dropped overboard.

Meanwhile the captain was standing above the stairs to the crew's cabin. "Mr. Gray!" he called to a sailor who might still be loyal. "I'm leaving this ship, and I order you to follow your captain. You have thirty seconds!"

There was a sudden scuffle and the sound of blows. Then Gray shot up the stairs. "I'm with you, Captain!" he gasped.

With that, we all piled into the rowboat. As we rowed away, the five

sailors left on board ran to the ship's cannon. Meanwhile some of the mutineers on shore had jumped into one of their boats. It looked as though they would try to head us off. The rest were probably running through the woods.

We rowed for dear life. Just as we got around the point and near the shore, a cannon ball came whizzing though the air. Whoosh! It landed just behind the boat, creating a huge wave that swamped us. Suddenly we were all standing up in three feet of water!

There was nothing for it but to grab what we could carry, and run for the stockade.

We could hear voices coming nearer. We stopped to load our guns. Just before we reached our goal, out of the trees came Job Anderson at the head of six mutineers. We opened fire, and one of them fell. That was enough. The rest ran back into the wood.

## Inside the Stockade

As we climbed over the fence, a sniper's bullet whistled by my ear. Poor Redruth, who was in front of me, was hit. The squire knelt beside him, but before he could finish a short prayer, his old servant was dead.

The first thing the captain did was raise the Union Jack. "That'll show them we mean business," he said. All the same, he was worried about how long our supplies would last.

We were still being bombarded by the occasional cannon ball. The captain remained perfectly calm. He got out his log and, as was his duty, began recording the events of the day. He hadn't got very far, though, before we heard a shout. The next thing we knew, Jim Hawkins was climbing over the stockade!

# Jim Once Again Tells his Story

When Ben Gunn saw the British flag flying above the trees on dry land, he stopped me.

"Your friends must have reached the stockade. If it were Silver, he'd be flying the pirate's black flag," said Ben. "Run along, boy, and tell the squire that Ben Gunn has something to propose. He can find me where you and I met."

Just then, cannonballs began flying overhead. I ran from tree to tree, and soon found myself near the beach.

I could see the black pirate's flag waving above the ship. The mutineers had lit a big fire on shore. They were shouting and laughing like children, and I figured they had been drinking rum.

Feeling safe for the moment, I ran back toward the stockade. How glad my friends were to see me!

Captain Smollet kept everyone busy. We were divided into two groups, one to keep watch while the other slept. In the meantime, he gave us jobs to do. We buried poor Redruth. Then I was sent to gather firewood, while the doctor was put in charge of cooking our meals.

I told them about my adventure with Ben Gunn, but forgot to mention something. Ben had told me he'd built a small boat, and that it was hidden near a white rock. Now I remembered seeing a white rock as I ran from the beach to the stockade.

## THE TRUCE

The next morning, who should turn up but Long John Silver with one of his men holding a white flag of truce. The man helped him over the fence. The captain ordered us to stay inside, then allowed Silver to speak.

"That was a good trick you pulled last night," said Long John, "but one poor fellow is done for."

Ben Gunn must have been up to something, I thought gleefully.

The captain had no idea what Long John was talking about, but you would never have guessed it. He said, "Well?" very calmly, and began to smoke a pipe.

After much talk, Long John finally asked for the map straight out. "I'll see that you're landed safely at the first port," he promised.

The captain was pretty sure that a pirate's promise was worth nothing.

"You have only one choice, Silver," he said sternly. "You and your men must surrender. You're stuck in that harbor. You can't sail the ship, and we'll never give you the map. If you won't surrender, we'll fight you to the last man!"

Long John was furious. "You've seen the last of me!" he shouted. He hobbled back toward the fence. Halfway there, he stopped and spat into our little spring. "There, that's what I think of you!"

His mate helped him over the fence, and he stumbled off, swearing terrible oaths as he disappeared into the wood.

# THE BATTLE

No sooner was Long John gone than Captain Smollet began getting us organized. He knew the mutineers would attack soon.

"Have your breakfast, Jim," he ordered, "and then be ready to load guns for us."

Shortly afterward, he called us all together. "Men," said he, "I've given Silver an answer that will make him attack us within the hour. We're outnumbered, but we have a strong position. It's better to fight now than to wait until our supplies run low."

We had little time to think about our danger. Before we knew it, a band of screeching pirates ran out of the woods and headed for the stockade. The squire and Gray were ready, and shot three men, but four of the others swarmed over the fence like monkeys.

Shots kept flying at us out of the woods. We retreated into the log cabin, pushing our guns through the loopholes and shooting.

One of the attackers crept up to the cabin, grabbed the barrel of Hunter's gun as it stuck out, and shoved it backward. Poor Hunter, standing inside, was knocked backward and fell senseless on the floor.

We could see Job Anderson peering over the fence, roaring, "At'em boys! At'em!" The next thing we knew, a pirate was at the doorway, attacking Dr. Livesey with a sword.

I heard pistol shots, then the captain's voice. "Out, lads, out, and fight'em in the open!"

There was a pile of swords on the floor, ready for emergencies. I grabbed one and rushed out, just in time to see the doctor knock down a pirate and slash him across the face.

"Round the house, lads, round the house!" cried the captain. I did as I was told, and ran around the corner of the house. Next moment I was face to face with Anderson. With a shout, he raised his sword.

I hadn't time to be afraid. In a flash, I dodged to one side, tripped in the sand, and went rolling head-over-heels down the slope. Gray, who had been right behind me, killed Anderson with one big slash of his sword.

Suddenly, the pirates seemed to lose heart. Those who were left scrambled back over the stockade and made off into the woods.

# My Sea Adventure

We were soon back in the log cabin. The captain was wounded, but not seriously. Poor Hunter's chest had been crushed and his skull fractured, and sometime in the night he died.

Once we had settled down again, the doctor said he was going to find Ben Gunn. He climbed the stockade and walked away into the cool shadows of the wood.

Inside the stockade, the sun beat down. The cabin got hotter by the minute. I went about my work feeling quite jealous of the doctor.

Suddenly, a brilliant idea came into my head. I would find out what the pirates were up to! Of course, it was pretty foolish of me, but I was thrilled with my plan.

I stuffed my pockets full of biscuits, and quietly picked up a couple of pistols while the squire and Gray were busy with the captain. I slipped out of the cabin, then bolted over the stockade and into the trees.

As quickly as I could, I crept along the shore. It took a long time, but at last I could see the ship. Two men, one wearing a red cap, were standing on the deck.

Long John was in a lifeboat beside the ship. His parrot, Cap'n Flint, sat on his shoulder screeching horribly. After a while, he rowed toward the beach. It looked as if most of the pirates were settled on shore.

The sun was sinking by the time I found the white rock. I discovered the boat in a small hollow, hidden by tall grass. It was made of goatskin stretched over a wood frame – just like the little boats called coracles, used by country folk in England. It was very light, and I managed to carry it to the water's edge without any trouble.

Ben's coracle was steered with a small paddle. At first all I did was turn round and round. The tide carried me straight toward the ship. As this was what I wanted, I soon gave up trying to paddle.

In a little while, the ship loomed up before me in the darkness. My plan was to find the anchor-rope – what the sailors called the hawser. As my little boat slipped by, I grabbed it.

The hawser was straining as the ship pulled with the tide. I waited until a puff of wind pushed the ship the other way. The rope was looser, now. I pulled out my little knife and cut almost all the way through the rope.

All this time I had heard the sound of loud voices from the back of the ship, where the captain's cabin was. Now I began to pay attention. One was Israel Hands. I guessed that the other was the sailor with the red cap.

They were plainly drunk, and angry as well. They were swearing at each other, and every so often a bottle would sail through the cabin window. On shore, I could see the red light of the pirates' campfire. The men were singing a mournful song:

*But one man of her crew alive,*
*What put to sea with seventy-five.*

Finally, there was another puff of wind, and the ship moved so that I could cut the last bit of anchor-rope.

At the same time, my little boat began to spin slowly around. It hit the side of the ship and slipped toward the rear. A dangling rope brushed my hand.

I grabbed it. Why I would do such a thing, I'll never know. But I hoisted myself up, hooked a foot on a cross-bar of my little boat, and peered into the cabin window.

One glance was enough. Hands and his companion were locked in a deadly struggle, each trying to strangle the other. I dropped back down into my little boat, still holding the rope.

It was then I realized that the ship was beginning to float out to sea on the tide! I could hear the pirates on shore behind me as I floated away:

> *Fifteen men on the dead man's chest –*
> *Yo-ho-ho, and a bottle of rum!*
> *Drink and the devil had done for the rest –*
> *Yo-ho-ho, and a bottle of rum!*

I let go of the rope pretty quickly, I can tell you. But the tide swept me along just as fast as the ship. All I could do was lie down flat in the bottom of the coracle and pray.

For hours I lay there, expecting to be dashed against a rock at any moment. At last, I fell fast asleep.

# The Cruise of the Coracle

It was broad daylight when I woke. My little boat was tossing in the waves at the southwest end of Treasure Island. The sun was beating down, and I began to feel terribly thirsty and very frightened.

When I peered over the edge, all I could see were tall cliffs and rocks sticking out of the water. Huge, slimy monsters were crawling around on the rocks. Every once in a while I could hear them bark. Then, plop! they'd fall into the sea. I later discovered these were sea lions, and pretty harmless. Right then, they seemed terrifying.

As long as I lay on the bottom, the coracle bobbed along on the current without any trouble. The minute I sat up and tried to steer, I would hit a wave and get badly splashed.

My only hope was to paddle once or twice every so often, while crouching low in the boat, and then to lie on the bottom again.

I was gradually working my way toward the shore when suddenly I looked up. There, a little in front of me, was the ship!

The *Hispaniola*'s sails gleamed in the sunshine, but it seemed to be turning in circles. I paddled as hard as I dared, trying to catch up with the ship. It was my only hope.

Just at that moment the wind changed. It filled the ship's sails and brought it around. It was coming straight at me! Hardly knowing what I was doing, I stood up.

As the coracle rose to

the top of a wave, I jumped for the boom sticking out from the ship's bow. I clung to it like a monkey. There was a sickening thump as the ship smashed my little boat.

Still terrified, I crawled along the boom and onto the deck. A gruesome sight met my eyes. There was blood splattered on the deck. Red Cap lay stiff as a poker on the boards. Israel Hands was slumped beside him, moaning.

"Welcome aboard, Mr. Hands," said I mockingly, remembering how he'd wanted to kill us all.

He rolled his eyes. "Brandy!" he gasped.

I ran down to the captain's cabin. The place was a mess – dirty fingerprints everywhere, heaps of empty bottles, and the furniture all topsy-turvy.

I rummaged around in the cupboards, and found a half-empty bottle of brandy for Hands. For myself, I took some biscuits and fruit.

"Are you much hurt?" I asked Hands. I gave him his brandy, and he drank it all.

"If that doctor were here, he'd have me fixed up in a minute," he grunted. "My friend here is dead as a doornail, and that's that! Say, where'd you come from, anyhow?"

"Never you mind," I retorted, "I've come aboard to take possession of this ship, and you're to consider me as captain from now on."

With that, I went to look for a proper flag. I took down the pirate's flag and chucked it overboard. Soon, the Union Jack was fluttering from the mast.

"God save the king!" I shouted.

Israel Hands looked at me slyly. "I reckon you'd like to get back to shore. Look here, if you give me food and drink, and a bandage for this wound in my leg, I'll tell you how to sail the ship. Is it a deal?"

It sounded good to me, and in three minutes I had the *Hispaniola* sailing easily before the wind. We skimmed along, heading for the North Inlet, far away from the pirate camp.

As our anchor was gone, we'd have to beach the ship. This meant waiting until the tide was well in. Hands showed me how to slow the ship down and lash the tiller. After a few tries, I succeeded.

I brought some food, and we sat eating, not saying a word.

Finally, he asked me if I'd be ready to heave the dead man overboard. I refused.

"Well," he said, "it isn't a pleasant sight, but no matter. Could you just step into the cabin and get me a – umm – a bottle of wine? This brandy's a bit too strong."

Hands eyes wandered as he spoke. I knew perfectly well he wanted me to leave the deck, but I couldn't imagine why. "All right," I said, "but it'll take some time."

With that, I scurried down the stairway as noisily as I could. Then, taking off my shoes, I ran quietly to the front of the ship and came up by another stairway.

I peered over the railing, and what should I see but Israel Hands, crawling along the deck! He picked up a long knife from a coil of rope, hid it in his jacket, then crawled back.

"He won't kill me until I've beached the ship safely," I thought. I tiptoed back, then clattered noisily up the stairs with the wine.

The tide was nearly full. Now I began the tricky business of steering through the narrow channel into the North Inlet. We could see the wreck of a three-masted ship by the shore.

"There's a fine bit of sand to beach the ship," said Hands, pointing to a spot beside the wreck. "Steady – now swing about!"

I whirled the wheel, and the ship began to turn slowly. In the excitement of steering, I forgot my danger. Something – perhaps a creak or a moving shadow – made me turn my head.

There was Hands, his knife raised to strike!

Our eyes met, and we both cried out, I in terror, he in fury. As he hurled himself forward, I jumped to one side and let go of the wheel. It spun, and one of the handles hit Hands in the chest.

At that moment, the *Hispaniola* struck the sand and fell to one side. The deck was at an angle, and we both slid down toward the railings.

In a second I stood up and jumped onto one of the tilting masts, climbing as fast as I could. Hands' knife shuddered into the wood just below me. He started climbing too, but very slowly, because of his wounded leg.

I still had my two pistols, and now I carefully loaded them both. "One more step, Mr. Hands, and I'll blow your brains out!"

He stopped instantly. "Jim," he said, "I reckon you've won, and I'll have to surrender."

I was smiling, very pleased with myself, when suddenly his right hand flashed back. Something sang like an arrow through the air, and I felt a sharp pain. I was pinned by the shoulder to the mast!

Before I knew it, I had squeezed the triggers of both pistols. They fell into the water below, and with them went Israel Hands, head first into the sea.

## Captain of the Ship

I could see Hands lying in the sand below the clear water. His dagger seemed to burn into my shoulder, and I felt sick and dizzy. In fact, the dagger had only caught the skin. As I tried to loosen the metal, my skin tore, and I was free.

I was so used to wild adventures by this time that nothing seemed to scare me. I calmly took the dead Red Cap by the waist, like a sack of potatoes, and tumbled him overboard. The two pirates lay side by side, with little fishes flitting above them.

After this, I bandaged my wound as best I could, then waded ashore. I walked quietly through the woods, looking cautiously from side to side the whole time. As I got close to the stockade, I saw an immense glow in the sky.

I stopped, feeling uneasy. The captain had never let us build big fires. But then came the sound of snoring, and I felt reassured. I climbed over the fence and peered into the cabin.

Suddenly a voice screeched, "Pieces of eight! Pieces of eight!" It was Long John's parrot! I tried to run.

Too late! Long John and his men jumped up. I ran right into one of them, and he held me so tight I could hardly breathe.

"Get a light!" Long John yelled.

Five pirates stood in front of me, their faces red from alcohol. A sixth was lying down, and looked deathly pale. The parrot sat on Long John's shoulder. Long John himself was looking pretty awful.

"Well, well!" he exclaimed. "If it isn't Jim Hawkins! Just dropped in for a visit? I call that downright friendly of you."

He sat on a rum barrel, took out a pipe, and lit it. "So here you are. I knew you were a smart boy the first time I set eyes on you. You're a lad of spirit, and I've always liked you. Dr. Livesey's pretty mad at you, so you'd better join us."

Then Long John explained that Dr. Livesey had gone to the pirate camp with a flag of truce. "An ungrateful scamp, that's what he called you. He also said our ship was gone, and so it was!"

Dr. Livesey had struck a bargain. The stockade and all it contained were handed over to the pirates, while Squire Trelawney and his party were free to move out unharmed. Long John had no idea where they were.

"Now choose," he said, turning to me again.

"Well," I said, "Here you are, ship lost, treasure lost, men lost. Who did it? I did! I was in that apple barrel when you planned the mutiny. I was the one who cut the ship's anchor-rope!"

Here I stopped to catch my breath. "I've got the ship safely ashore where none of you will ever find it. Kill me if you like! But if you spare me, I'll forget all your mischief and try to save you from being hanged when we get back to London."

They all sat looking at me like sheep. Then the men began muttering, and went out of the cabin. Long John and I were left alone.

"Now see here, Jim," whispered Long John. "That lot want to kill you and get rid of me as their captain. I'll save your life if I can, and you must save me from hanging when we get back."

It all seemed impossible, but I whispered, "All right."

He smiled. "By the way, the doctor gave me the map."

# THE BLACK SPOT AGAIN

I barely had time to take in the astounding news when the men returned from their meeting. The five of them stood in the doorway, hesitating.

"Come on, I won't eat you!" said Long John.

The youngest of the mutineers stepped forward, handed something to Long John, then stepped back nervously.

"The black spot," said Long John. "I thought so. Well, you'll all hang now."

"We don't want you for our captain any more," said one of the men. "First, you've made a mess of this treasure hunt. Second, you let the enemy go for no good reason. Third, you wouldn't let us attack them afterwards. And then there's the boy."

"Is that all?" asked Long John calmly.

"It's enough," answered the pirate.

Long John snorted. "What a bunch of fools you are. Don't you understand? That boy is the only way we can save our skins!"

He paused for a moment. "And don't you think it better to have a live doctor around when we're suffering from marsh fever?"

With that, he took out the map from his pocket and threw it on the ground. The pirates jumped forward and grabbed it, shouting for joy.

"Yes, that's Flint's writing!" cried one.

"Silver for captain!" shouted another. That settled the matter.

Next morning the doctor paid them a visit. When Long John told him I was there, he asked to speak to me.

"Doctor," replied Long John, "the boy will tell you how I saved his life at the risk of my own. Say you'll save mine in return!"

The doctor nodded. "Silver, I wouldn't count on that treasure. If we get out of this mess alive, I'll put in a good word for you."

"So Jim," said Dr. Livesey, "here you are. It wasn't right of you to run off, especially when Captain Smollet was wounded."

I must confess I began to cry when he reproached me like this. "I've blamed myself bitterly enough," I said through my tears. "If Long John hadn't stood up for me, I'd be dead by now. But there's another thing. I know where the ship is."

"Good heavens, Jim!" he exclaimed when I told him of my sea adventure. "It seems you're a guardian angel in disguise." He shook my hand warmly, waved to Long John, and left.

Next morning the pirates rushed around making excited preparations for the treasure hunt. What a strange procession we made in our dirty, torn clothes!

Everyone but me was armed to the teeth, or carried shovels, pickaxes, and food. Long John had tied a rope to my belt and led me along like a puppy dog. The parrot sat on his shoulder, squawking and swearing.

# Hunting for Treasure

The pirates were soon squabbling among themselves. The first argument was over the treasure map. The red cross was not a very exact guide. On the back of the map, Flint had written, "Tall tree, Spyglass shoulder, north-northeast. Skeleton Island, east-southeast. Ten feet."

Long John seemed better at figuring out which tall tree it should be, once we got near the spot. He told the men to fan out as we climbed a steep hill. Soon came a shout.

At the foot of a big pine lay a human skeleton, covered in vines. Its feet pointed toward Skeleton Island.

"Just Flint's idea of a joke," said Long John, checking his compass. "That skeleton is pointing east-south east."

The men bunched together, looking scared. "That was one of our mates in the old days. Flint must have killed him in cold blood," they muttered, looking around uneasily. I could see they were very superstitious.

At that very moment, an eerie sound rang out, echoing through the trees:

*Fifteen men on the dead man's chest –*
*Yo-ho-ho and a bottle of rum!*

"It's Flint!" shouted the men, turning pale.

"Nonsense," snapped Long John. "Flint died of drink in Savannah. He's dead and buried for sure." The pirates didn't budge.

"Let's get out of here!" cried one, his teeth chattering. "I don't like ghosts."

"Ghosts? Ghosts' voices don't echo," said Long John. "That didn't sound like Flint's voice, anyway. It sounded more like . . . "

"Ben Gunn!" shouted one of the old-time pirates.

"You're right!" exclaimed Long John.

"But he's dead too," said another. "Anyway, nobody minds Ben Gunn, dead or alive!"

The men laughed, although I thought they still sounded pretty nervous. We staggered on through the pines that grew on the hill.

The men were silent now, their minds on the fabulous treasure that lay ahead somewhere. Even Long John tugged at me roughly if I lagged behind.

Before we had gone very far, however, the men suddenly stopped. In front of us was a huge hole. It had been dug some time ago, because grass had sprouted at the bottom. Inside it lay a broken axe and some boxes marked *Walrus,* the name of Flint's ship.

Someone had found the treasure site and taken everything!

I was amazed at how Long John kept his head, faced with this terrible disappointment.

"Jim," he whispered, handing me a double-barreled pistol, "take that, and stand by for trouble."

Swearing and shouting, the men started to dig with their fingers.

"Is that your treasure?" yelled one, holding up a gold piece.

"Dig away, boys," said Long John, as cool as you please. "I wouldn't be surprised if you found some peanuts."

"Peanuts!" screeched the other, beside himself with rage. "Mates, do you hear that? He knew all along there wasn't anything here!"

The men glared at us. Long John stared right back at them.

The ringleader started to shout, "Let's kill'em, mates – "

He never finished his sentence. There was a rattle of gunfire from the trees. One man went down, and three others took to their heels. Crack! This time it was Long John's pistol, and the ringleader lay dead in the hole.

At the same moment, the doctor, Gray, and Ben Gunn joined us, and we all started chasing the three escaped pirates, afraid they might get to the lifeboats. But soon we spotted them running in the opposite direction.

We rowed around to North Inlet. Leaving Gray to guard the *Hispaniola,* we walked up the hill to Ben's cave. There we found Captain Smollet lying by a big fire. Beside him were heaps of coins and gold bars.

"Come in, Jim," said the captain kindly. "You're a good boy, but I don't think we'll go to sea together again. You have too many adventures for my taste!"

Then the doctor told us Ben's story.

The marooned man had finally found the treasure and had carried it, bit by bit, to a cave on the north side of the island. He'd told the doctor about it, and had offered his cave as a refuge.

It was after this that the doctor and his friends made their bargain with the pirates, and gave Long John the map. They'd kept an eye on the mutineers inside the stockade, though, and that's how they managed to turn up just in the nick of time.

"Jim, I'm glad to see you safe and sound," said the squire kindly. "As for you, John Silver, you're a monstrous rascal! And they tell me I'm to let you go free instead of being hanged!"

"Thank you kindly, sir," replied Long John without a blush.

## THE RETURN

We began loading the treasure onto the ship the next day. On the third evening, we heard a sound like shrieking or singing.

"The mutineers!" said the doctor. "Perhaps I should go to them."

"Sir, they'd kill you in a minute," warned Long John.

In the end, we decided to leave them a good supply of gun powder and weapons for hunting, as well as food, clothing, and tools.

As we sailed away, we saw them kneeling on the beach, begging for help. The doctor shouted that we'd left supplies, but they put a bullet through our sails just the same.

As Treasure Island disappeared behind us, we made plans to land at a port in Mexico and find a new crew to sail the ship across the Atlantic.

We dropped anchor in a beautiful bay and went ashore, leaving Ben and Long John on the boat. By the time our business was finished it was dark.

Ben Gunn was alone when we boarded the *Hispaniola* again. Trembling, he told us that Long John had gone. "I let him go, because I'm sure he'd have killed us all in the end." Ever true to his nature, Long John had stolen a sack of gold to take with him.

As for the rest of us, we shared the gold, and I went home to my mother a happy fellow, cured forever of wanting to hunt for buried treasure!

# THE END

© 1991 Dami Editore, Italy
Illustrated by Libico Maraja
Text by Jane Brierley based on
an adaptation by S. Pazienza

Published in 1994 by
Tormont Publications Inc.
338 Saint Antoine St. East
Montreal, Canada  H2Y 1A3

ISBN 2-89429-587-1

Printed in EEC, Officine Grafiche De Agostini - Novara 1994
Bound by Legatoria del Verbano S.p.A.